Young Merlin

by

Tony Bradman

Illustrated by Nelson Evergreen

First published in 2009 in Great Britain by
Barrington Stoke Ltd
18 Walker St, Edinburgh, EH3 7LP

This edition first published 2012

www.barringtonstoke.co.uk

ISBN: 978-1-78112-072-9

Printed in China by Leo

Contents

1   Not Like Other Boys   1

2   Meeting the King   9

3   Blood on the Stones   19

4   The Cave of Wisdom   30

5   A Brand New Beginning   40

Chapter 1
Not Like Other Boys

Merlin woke suddenly and sat up. He didn't know what time it was but it was still very dark. His heart was pounding as if it wanted to explode. His eyes were wide open too, but he could see nothing around him, only the terrible things he'd been dreaming about.

"Blood and death! I can't stand any more blood and death," he moaned. He shook all over, and he felt sick. His skin hurt too –

almost as if it was being burned off by great waves of fire. "Teeth and tails, the red and the white ..."

Suddenly a flame lit up the dark around him. What could it be? He looked up – the flame was only a candle. And it was his mother who'd lit it. He was in the hut he and his mother lived in. She came over and sat next to him on his rush bed, with the candle in her hand.

"There, there, everything's all right now," she said. She stroked his face with her hand. "You're so hot! Was it the same old nightmare?"

"I ... I think so," said Merlin as his heart slowed down. His mother's hand felt cool on his cheek, and he saw her smile in the candle-light.

"Oh, well, it's gone now," she said. "It's a shame you can never remember any of your nightmares. Maybe if you told me what it's about you wouldn't have it so often ... It might make it a bit less scary, too."

Merlin had had the same nightmare many times, ever since he'd been small. But now it came much more often, and left him more upset. So he was glad he couldn't remember very much of it once he was awake.

"Don't worry, Mother," he said. "You can go back to bed now. I'll be fine."

"If you're sure ..." she said, and looked into his eyes for a moment. "You know, you're very special, Merlin. Now sleep tight and don't have any dreams at all."

Merlin fell asleep again at last, but it took a long time. That word *special* kept going round and round in his mind. He was still thinking about it when he woke up in the morning, and it stayed stuck in his head while he ate his thin porridge. His mother was upset to see her son's gloomy face. She sent him off to fetch a bucket of milk.

It was a damp, cloudy autumn day, and Merlin plodded through the village, feeling worried. He lived with his mother in the far west of Britain. The country around the village was full of steep mountains and deep valleys. They were poor, like all the people in the village, but his mother often told him he was special.

He had no father, but there were plenty of children like him whose fathers had been killed or were away fighting. These were difficult, dangerous times in Britain. Bands of Saxon warriors rode across the land, stealing and murdering, and many Britons were killed in battles with them.

But Merlin had never had a father. Merlin's mother said that he had just ... arrived. Her own family were rich and important. No one had believed her when she'd said her baby had no father. She couldn't tell them anything more, so they had kicked her out and sent her to live far away. Everyone in the village knew the story of Merlin and his mother. Merlin hated the way people pointed at her and laughed. They made jokes about her too.

But he hated the way they thought of him even more. The village grown-ups had always been horrible. They whispered and muttered to each other when they thought he wasn't listening. And the children were worse – they called him names and didn't even play with him.

Merlin was at the edge of the village now. He stopped at the farm where he got the milk. There was a full barrel of milk by the door of the cowshed and a big wooden spoon. He spooned milk into his bucket as the cows mooed at him from the warm gloom of the shed. He left a coin in payment. The farmer and his wife gave him nasty looks from the door of their cottage.

"Go on, be off with you," the farmer growled. He held out his hand with the fingers in the shape of a devil's horns. It was the sign to defend himself and his wife against The Evil Eye – the villagers always made it when they saw Merlin. There was something about him that made them feel very nervous.

Merlin set off home with the bucket of milk. If only he was normal! He often thought he'd give a lot to be like the rest of the boys in the village. But deep inside he felt his mother was right. He knew he *was* different in some way. It was no good trying to pretend he wasn't. The dream told him that, even if he never remembered what happened in it. There were other things as well –

strange, scary things he thought about that he kept secret from his mother.

He pushed down the bad thoughts and walked on slowly. Maybe he could change and then people would like him more. Maybe if he was really nice to them, they would be a bit nicer to him ...

Just then, Merlin heard the sound of hooves pounding across the nearby fields. He looked up and saw a small band of warriors on horse-back galloping towards the village. As they came closer, Merlin saw where they wanted to go. Suddenly he went cold all over – they were heading straight for his hut! He dropped the bucket with a loud clang, and all the milk spilt onto the muddy path.

But Merlin didn't care. He was already running, calling out to his mother ...

Chapter 2
Meeting the King

The warriors stopped in front of the hut but they didn't get down from their horses. Merlin saw his mother come out and one of the riders said something to her. She shook her head, and seemed a bit puzzled, but she didn't look all that worried.

"Is this the boy?" said the man as Merlin ran up and stood next to his mother, taking her hand in his. The man stared down at Merlin with cold, hard eyes.

Merlin watched the warriors on their tall war horses. There were ten of them and each wore fine chainmail and a helmet with a red crest. All of them had spears and swords which shone in the light. "Yes, this is my son," said Merlin's mother and pulled him close to her. "But I'm afraid you'll have to tell me again. Er ... what exactly do you want with him?"

"It's not me who wants him," the man answered with a scowl. "We are the body-guards of Great King Vortigern who is ruler of Britain. We have been sent to find the boy and bring him back to the King's fortress. We've ridden all night to get here."

"But why?" said Merlin's mother. "It's not every day that the King summons a boy from a poor village. Even though I know Merlin *is* special ..."

"Mother!" Merlin hissed. He began to blush. All ten warriors were staring at him now, looking right into his face. "I wish you wouldn't say that!"

"The King has reasons for wanting the boy," said the man with a shrug and his horse snorted as if it agreed. "No more talking now," he went on. "We have a long, hard ride ahead of us."

"Well, I can't understand it," said Merlin's mother. "I suppose it could be something good." She turned to Merlin. "It's up to you, Merlin. Do you want to go?" she asked.

Merlin looked at her, and then at the warriors. He was scared, of course, but excited as well. Part of him hated the idea that this would mark him out even more and make him look less normal than ever. But another part of him felt there was something right about it, something that made sense.

"I do," he said, and the sun broke through the clouds and shone down on him.

His mother smiled and kissed him, and the warrior who had spoken reached out to Merlin and swung the boy up onto the saddle in front of him. Then the warrior wheeled his horse round and galloped away, with the others following. Merlin waved to his mother, but the village was soon left behind.

The leader of the King's body-guards had been right – it *was* a long, hard journey. They rode through thick forest and over mountains that looked as if the bones of giants lay under the land. They crossed wild moors and forded rivers of cold, clear water. They swept past villages and towns, many of them in ruins. The steady gallop of the warrior's horse almost lulled Merlin to sleep. But he kept himself awake and tried to remember everything he had heard about Vortigern.

The King was a great man, of course, but no one liked him. He had taken power when the Roman Empire in the west had fallen. The Romans had left the Britons to look after themselves and King Vortigern had promised to protect the people from the raiders and pirates who had attacked the Romans and at last sent them back to Rome. Vortigern had a clever plan. At least it had seemed clever at the time ... The raiders were terrific warriors, and the Saxons were the best of all of them. Vortigern paid a lot of Saxon soldiers to join his army and fight the other raiders off. But the Saxons betrayed him. They turned against him and a new war began.

The Saxons wanted to make Britain their own country, and the war they unleashed was long and bitter. Vortigern had stopped the Saxons for a while, but the people of Britain had paid a terrible price. And the Saxons still hadn't gone away. They had stolen most of the rich, eastern part of Britain, and kept it.

"Are you awake, boy?" said the warrior holding Merlin. "We're here."

Merlin had guessed that already. They had at last arrived in a beautiful valley with mountains all around it. A large, strong-looking fortress stood at the far end, perched on a rocky slope above the valley floor. As they got closer, Merlin could see the fortress wasn't finished. Part of it even seemed to have fallen down.

But there was no time for him to see more. The sun was starting to set as they rode into a camp that filled one side of the valley. More warriors sat in front of their tents, or huddled round fires, talking in low voices. None of them seemed happy, and Merlin felt them all stare at him as he went by.

The King's body-guards stopped by a large tent in the middle of the camp, and got off their horses. Merlin was pushed inside and the warrior jabbed a spear into his back each time he took a step.

"My lord, I bring the boy you ordered us to seek," said the warrior with a bow.

Merlin looked hard at the man who was sitting on a throne in the tent. So this was the Great King, ruler of Britain. Vortigern was dark and brooding. He wore fine clothes and had a slim band of gold around his head. He leant forward keenly to listen to what the warrior said and his eyes glittered in the candle light, his face full of hope.

"Are you sure?" Vortigern said. "Is this the boy who has no father?"

"Yes, my lord," said the warrior. He glanced down at the boy beside him, and

Merlin saw a quick flash of pity in his eyes. Merlin began to feel uneasy.

"Excellent," said Vortigern with an evil smile. "Prepare him for the sacrifice!"

Merlin gulped. Perhaps coming here hadn't been such a good idea after all …

Chapter 3
Blood on the Stones

A strange, terrifying man suddenly stepped out of the shadows behind the King, and grabbed Merlin with his long, thin fingers. He was like something from a nightmare – horrible and old with mad, staring eyes and dirty white hair and a beard. He wore a long, filthy black cloak with a hood ... and he smelt of death. There were others behind him, a crowd of men who looked like giant crows.

The Romans had made Britain a Christian country before they had left. But in these difficult times Merlin knew many people had turned to the old gods of magic and blood, the ones that had been worshipped long before the Romans came. The man who'd grabbed Merlin's arm was a druid, a priest of the old gods, and the others were druids too. Merlin knew now that he was in deep, deep trouble.

"Hey, let go of me!" he yelled as he fought to free himself. "No one said anything about a sacrifice. I wouldn't have come here if I'd known that!"

"Silence, boy!" screamed the King. He stood up and pointed at him. "You'll do what you're told! I have to kill you to save my kingdom."

"Why?" Merlin asked. "You can't just kill me without telling me why!" He needed time.

The druid was too strong, and he couldn't shake him off. Merlin had to think of a way to escape. "I might be happier if I knew what this was all about," he said. "And then I'd make a better sacrifice then, wouldn't I?"

"Umm, good point ..." said Vortigern, sitting down again. He looked worried.

"I want to make sure the sacrifice won't fail," Vortigern growled. He pointed at the druid. "Go on then, tell him!" he shouted.

The old man let go of Merlin, and scowled at him. Merlin rubbed his arms where the druid's hard, bony fingers had dug into his flesh, and scowled back. At least he wasn't being held any more.

"Last summer, when the war with the Saxons came to an end at long last, our Great King Vortigern planned to build a new fortress here in this valley," the druid began. "But every time the walls are as high as a man, the ground begins to shake and the walls fall down again. We think there's a curse on the land ..."

"And you can guess how annoying *that* is," Vortigern muttered. He shifted in his throne and nervously chewed a thumb nail. "I mean, I badly need that fortress to be built! How can I protect myself from the Saxons if I don't have a really strong fortress to live in? They're out to kill all Britons – even me!"

You should protect your people, thought Merlin, *not yourself.* He frowned, but didn't say a word. He waited for the druid to carry on. He kept on looking around the tent for a way out, an escape. The leader of the body-guards was still behind him, but Merlin thought he might just have a chance of making it out through the door of the tent. But he would have to be quick. Then what? The whole of Vortigern's army was in the valley, standing between him and freedom. How would he get past them?

"I am the High Priest of the Druids. King Vortigern, our lord and master, asked me to find out how to stop the walls from falling," said the druid. "I told him that we need a sacrifice, a boy of noble birth who has no father. We must kill such a boy and pour his blood on the stones of the fortress walls. Then they will stand."

"Er ... hold on," said Merlin. "How did you know all that? How did you know the sacrifice had to be me? Is it written down somewhere?"

"As a matter of fact, it is!" snapped the druid with an angry frown. "We have chests full of old books and scrolls in the high temple, and it's written in one of those."

"All we had to do was find a boy with no father," said Vortigern. "And it didn't take long, thank goodness. I got some of my men to check with the noble families, and your name came up right away. Your grandparents didn't want to tell us about you, but we tracked you down in the end."

"I don't have any grandparents," muttered Merlin. He hated the people who had betrayed him to Vortigern. "Anyway, none that I have ever seen or met."

"Well, tut tut, I don't know what families are coming to these days," sneered the King. "That's exactly what they said about you. They said they didn't have a grandson. But their servants told my men all about you and your mother. Right, let's get on with it ..."

"To be honest, I'd rather give the whole sacrifice thing a miss," said Merlin. "If you don't mind, I'd quite like to keep my blood inside my body. I'm off! Bye!"

Then he turned and ran. He ducked under the druid's hands as the old man tried to grab him. The druid tripped over and fell with a crash and began to shout out curses, and Merlin shot out of the tent. The rest of the King's body-guards were waiting outside, but Merlin dashed past them before they could stop him.

"Don't just stand there, you idiots!" he heard Vortigern yell. "Catch that brat!"

Merlin ran even faster. He dodged between the tents, swerving round the out-stretched hands of the warriors who dived at him. There were more behind him, and he could sense them getting closer. He could almost feel them breathing down his neck.

He reached open ground at last, and saw the fortress dead ahead ... But that was no good – a crowd of warriors was running out of it, all after him. He quickly changed

direction and doubled back, heading for the valley.

That was no good either. Another crowd of warriors ran out at him from the other side of the camp, and Merlin saw he was trapped. And that's when he noticed it – a small black hole in the rocky hill just below the walls of the fortress.

Merlin stopped and thought about it for a second – and then he dived into the dark ...

Chapter 4
The Cave of Wisdom

It was the entrance to some sort of cave, and at first it was a very tight squeeze. Was it just a trap? But soon the space before him began to open out. He still couldn't see where he was going and he could hear King Vortigern's soldiers not far behind, their voices ringing from the walls. But at least he could stand up now and breathe.

Suddenly the ground began to shake, and he heard shouts of warning and screams of panic. There was a deep rumbling sound and a *CRASH!* followed by a weird stillness. The air was filled with dust. Merlin coughed as he worked out that the noise had been more of the fortress falling down. That meant he was trapped in the cave.

The darkness was all around him. It seemed to press in on him, and for a moment Merlin began to feel panic. But then he calmed down. At least he was safe for the time being. The King and his evil druid couldn't get to him through all that rock. In any case, there must be another way out – he just had to keep going and find it. So he moved on, feeling for the cave wall beside him with his hands.

Slowly his eyes grew used to the darkness. He began to make out the shapes of the rocks around him and under his feet, and he saw there was a glimmer of light up ahead. He went round a bend – and stepped

into an enormous space – a cave taller than
the tallest tree, so big that Merlin couldn't
see to its far side. The light came from a
large pool of water in the cave floor. It was
almost the same size as a lake, and its water
had a weird sheen. Wisps of steam rose from
its smooth, silvery surface.

Merlin stood still, amazed to find such a
secret and magic place. But he had to find a
way out, and he started to scan the walls for
an exit. Suddenly the floor began to shake
again, and the water in the pool hissed and
bubbled. Big rocks tumbled from above,
crashing onto the floor of the cave. Merlin
dived for cover, crawling to the nearest wall
and huddling with his arms over his head.

Then something happened that made his
mouth fall open with shock. A dark shape
broke the surface of the pool and rose up –
and up, and up, and up, the gleaming water
running off its deep red scales. It was a

massive beast, and it had a long neck and an even longer tail. It had a powerful body, and legs like tree trunks. It had sharp fangs and hooked claws and great leathery wings.

Merlin knew what it was, of course, even though he had never seen one before. It was a dragon – and a large and impressive one, too. Merlin knew that few people were left alive if they ever met such a beast. He waited to be roasted to a crisp by a burst of flame, or perhaps the dragon was going to swallow him whole.

But the dragon did neither of those things. To Merlin's surprise, it bent its head down until its nose was almost touching Merlin's face. And then it spoke.

"You are here at last," it said and its voice was like thunder whispering. Grey smoke curled slowly from its enormous nostrils, and its giant yellow eyes were fixed

on Merlin's. "Why have you not come before? I have called to you many times ..."

"I ... I don't understand," said Merlin. He could feel the cave wall right up against his back, so he knew he couldn't get away. "What do you mean?"

"Do you not know this place?" said the dragon. Its breath smelt of winter fires, or the air when lightning strikes. "Have you not seen it in your dream?"

"My dream?" said Merlin. The dragon moved to the side, getting out of the boy's way so he could see the cavern once more. "Yes, you're right, I have ..."

As soon as the dragon had said it, Merlin remembered the beginning of the dream. It always started with him in the cave, standing by the pool of water.

"This is the Cave of Wisdom," said the dragon. "This is where your destiny has been waiting for you. Here you will see what will come in the future."

Merlin gasped. The air before him shimmered and he could see shadows moving in it, shapes that quickly turned into pictures of real things. He saw more Saxon ships land on the coasts of Britain. He saw the men from the ships swarm inland like a dark flood. He saw Vortigern's army march out to meet them. He saw villages burning, men fighting, great rivers of blood flowing through the burned and broken land. This was his dream – he saw blood and death for the people of Britain.

After a while the pictures changed. Now the armies grew faint as, out of the smoke, roared a huge white dragon. The cave rocked and shook as the red and white dragons fought. They growled and snarled and fired bursts of flame from their nostrils, and tore and ripped at each other with their fangs and claws. Merlin understood the red dragon stood for his people, the Britons, and the white dragon for the Saxons. And the battle between them seemed doomed to go on till the end of time ...

"Stop, I can't stand it any more!" yelled Merlin at last. The pictures were gone, the white dragon screaming with anger as it vanished. "Why did you make me dream of these things?" Merlin sobbed. "Why am I here? What has any of it got to do with *me?*"

"Because you have a part to play in what you have seen here," said the red dragon, its voice soft and kind now. "And deep down you have always known it."

"But what can *I* do?" Merlin whispered.

"Ah, you have far more in you than normal boys," said the dragon. "You have special powers. And they will all be set free ... when you bathe in the waters of the Cave of Wisdom."

Merlin looked deep into the dragon's yellow eyes, and saw two little pictures of himself reflected in them. Which Merlin should he be? The old, unhappy one? Or the strange new Merlin that this dragon seemed to offer him?

It was easy to choose. Merlin smiled, got to his feet, headed for the pool ...

Chapter 5
A Brand New Beginning

Merlin stepped into the glowing pool. The rock beneath his feet was smooth and he walked slowly down into the water. He kept walking until the water came up to his chin. It was warm, almost hot. He turned round at last and looked up at the red dragon.

"Is this all right?" the boy said. "Or is there something special I should do?"

"You must go deeper," said the dragon. "Let the water cover your head."

Merlin took a deep breath … and did what he was told. Suddenly he felt his skin begin to tingle all over. His mind began to open like a flower greeting the sun. His eyes were shut but it was as if he could see everything clearly. He understood how special he was. The forces of goodness had made him so that he could help his people when they were most in need.

It didn't matter any more that he had no father. He had a task to complete – a mission. He was sure he had the powers to make a good job of it, too. He knew now that his dark thoughts had been about what he was going to have to do. In his mind he had seen himself doing strange and terrible things and he had wanted to keep them secret from his mother. But soon it would be time to go and do them in the real world.

Merlin rose slowly from the pool and stood beside it. The silvery water dripped off his body. But it left a silver glow on his skin. When he looked down at his hands, he saw little blue sparks leap from the ends of his fingers. He pointed at the cave wall – and a flash like lightning darted from his fingertips and blasted a great big hole in the cave. Merlin laughed out loud. Even the old rags of his tunic had turned into the white gown of a wizard.

The red dragon put its head down close to Merlin. "Your powers are strong, but you will have to learn to use them wisely," it said. "You cannot defeat the Saxons alone, even with your special powers. The fight for this land of Britain will be long and hard, with many twists and turns. You will need to make the Britons work together. You will need some friends, too ..."

Merlin looked into the dragon's eyes and laid a hand on its enormous head. Its scales were smooth and cool. The great beast gave a sigh and blinked slowly. It purred and arched its back as if it was a huge cat that Merlin was stroking.

"Don't worry, I'll be careful," said Merlin. "I know what I have to do, and how difficult it will be. Thanks for your advice. For everything, in fact. I won't forget it. I'd like to think of you as a friend I might call on in the days and years ahead."

"I will always be here when you need me," said the red dragon.

"That's good to know," said Merlin. "Now I suppose I'd better get started. What is the best way out? I want to give Vortigern a surprise ..."

The King was still in his tent, shouting at the leader of his body-guards and at the old druid. Vortigern was very cross, and he was taking his anger out on them.

"I'm surrounded by total idiots!" he yelled. "I can't believe you let the brat escape! You'll both be killed if the boy is not back before the morning ..."

"Temper, temper," said a voice behind him. Vortigern whirled round and saw a slim figure standing in the entrance to the tent, a boy in a long white gown. "Don't you know who I am, Vortigern?" said the boy with an odd smile on his face.

"It's him!" the King screamed. "Quick, grab him before he can get away again!"

The chief of the body-guards and the old druid jumped forward. They ran at Merlin and behind them were even more warriors and druids out to get him once and for all. Merlin simply held up his hand – and it was as if they had all run right into a stone wall.

They fell onto their backs and lay there groaning. Vortigern screamed for help, and two more warriors ran into the tent with their spears held high. Again Merlin held up a hand – and fired a bolt of lightning at them. Soon they were on the ground groaning with the rest.

Vortigern stared at Merlin and slowly sank to his knees.

"Please don't hurt me!" he begged in a voice that whined and squeaked. "I'll make you rich!"

"On your feet, Vortigern," snapped Merlin. "I know you're not much of a king, but you could at least try to look like one. And I don't want to be rich."

"So what do you want?" said Vortigern. Everyone in the tent was listening.

"Well ... first I'd like something to eat and drink," said Merlin with a smile. "It's been a long day, and I haven't eaten a thing since I had my breakfast." The King snapped his fingers, and his servants rushed about to get a table and chair ready for this incredible young boy. Merlin went on. "When I've eaten, then I think you and I should have a chat. You picked the wrong place to build your new fortress ..."

****

Merlin made Vortigern give his mother a fine house to live in, and no one ever dared make jokes about her again. She wasn't surprised about her son's rise to fame and power.

"I always knew you were special, Merlin," she often said when he came to visit her.

"Mother!" Merlin always answered, blushing with embarrassment.

But he knew it was true.

Our books are tested
for children and young people by
children and young people.

Thanks to everyone who consulted on
a manuscript for their time and effort in
helping us to make our books better
for our readers.

See what happens next in ...

MERLIN
and the Ring of Power

by Tony Bradman

**In a time of myth and a land of magic,
one boy will shape the future...**

Merlin knows his destiny makes him different. His
power is growing every day. But there are other
threats to deal with.

The King.

And the Ring of Power Merlin must find
to save the land...